KENTUCKY

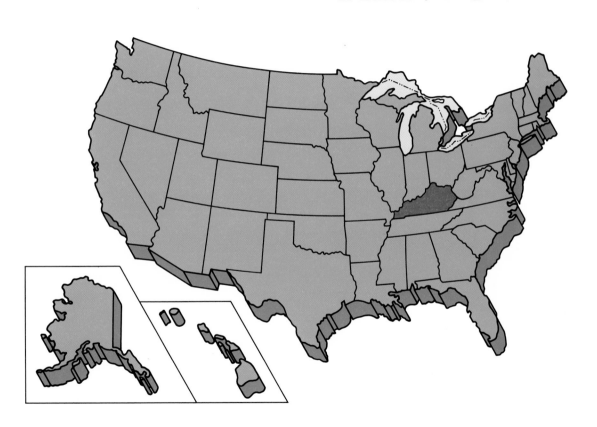

KENTUCKY

Dottie Brown

Lerner Publications Company

LIBRARY OF CONGRESS
CATALOGING-IN-PUBLICATION DATA
Brown, Dottie.
    Kentucky / Dottie Brown.
        p.   cm. – (Hello USA)
    Includes index.
    Summary: Introduces the geography, history, people, industries, and other highlights of Kentucky.
    ISBN 0–8225–2715–4 (lib. bdg.)
    1. Kentucky–Juvenile literature.
[1. Kentucky.] I. Title. II. Series.
F451.3.B76   1992
976.9–dc20   91–13057

Manufactured in the United States of America
2 3 4 5 6 7 8 9 10 – JR – 04 03 02 01 00 99 98 97 96

Cover photograph courtesy of Daniel E. Dempster © 1992.

The glossary that begins on page 68 gives definitions of words shown in **bold type** in the text.

CONTENTS

Did You Know . . . ?

❑ More than $6 billion worth of gold is held in the underground vaults of Fort Knox, Kentucky. This is the largest amount of gold stored anywhere in the world.

❑ The country's first cheeseburger was served in 1934 at Kaelin's Restaurant in Louisville, Kentucky.

❑ The public saw an electric light for the first time in Louisville. Thomas Edison introduced his incandescent light bulb to crowds at the Southern Exposition in 1883.

☐ If you visited Mammoth Cave National Park in Kentucky, you would be in the longest known cave system in the world. The cave has over 300 miles (483 kilometers) of mapped trails.

☐ When the moon is full, a moonbow appears in the mist created by Cumberland Falls in Kentucky. This nighttime display of colors has been seen nowhere else in the western half of the world.

Rainbows shine over Cumberland Falls during the day. At night, the light of the moon creates a similar arc of color.

A Trip Around the State

"Elbow room!" cried Daniel Boone, Kentucky's famous frontiersman. He had heard many stories about the wilderness that the Cherokee Indians called *Kentahteh,* meaning "land of tomorrow." Boone longed to settle in a place with open land and lots of game—and without lots of people. So he took a hunting trip to what is now Kentucky and decided to make it his home.

Boone and other settlers found more than open land in Kentucky. They also found giant caves, hardwood forests, tree-studded mountains, and wide rivers. Rivers form more than half of the state's boundaries. Beyond the borders lie Kentucky's neighboring states—Virginia, West Virginia, Ohio, Indiana, Illinois, Missouri, and Tennessee.

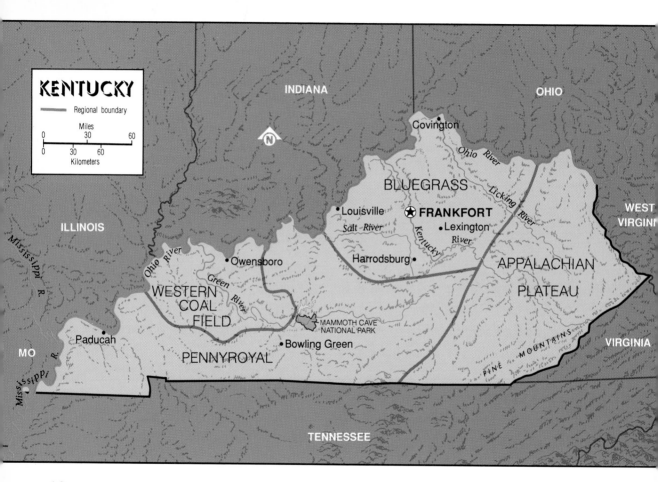

Kentucky's fertile land was formed millions of years ago, when an ancient sea flooded much of the state. Coral, shellfish, and sharks lived in the invading waters. When the ocean dried up, it left behind the shells and skeletons of the sea creatures. Over time, their remains decayed into a rich soil.

Another valuable resource developed in the ancient **swamps** that covered eastern and western Kentucky. Swampland plants died and began to rot. Layers of heavy soil collected above the decaying plants. Over millions of years, as the weight of the soil pressed the plants together, they changed into coal, a black substance used as fuel.

Cypress trees soak in the swamps of western Kentucky.

11

Coal deposits and fertile soil are only two of Kentucky's riches. The state's four land regions each have their own features and natural resources. In the east is the mountainous Appalachian Plateau. The tree-covered peaks of the Pine Mountains rise from the **plateau,** an area of high, flat land. Many steep valleys, rushing rivers, and winding streams cut through the region. One of Kentucky's two major coal deposits, the eastern coal field, lies beneath part of the Appalachian Plateau.

Forests blanket the rolling Appalachian Plateau, which covers more than one-fourth of the state.

Kentucky's nickname—the Bluegrass State—comes from a grass that thrives in the Bluegrass Region. The grass isn't really blue, but in the spring it grows tiny blue buds.

Kentucky's famous bluegrass and tobacco grow in the Bluegrass Region of north central Kentucky. Long wooden fences stretch across the area's grassy hills and mark the borders of horse farms. Sandy, conelike formations called **knobs** lie along the southern edge of the Bluegrass Region. This area is known as the Knobs.

13

Running water carved Mammoth Cave out of the limestone rock underneath the Pennyroyal Region.

The Pennyroyal Region sprawls along much of Kentucky's southern border, reaching north to the Knobs and west to Missouri. A barren area separates the Pennyroyal's flat farmland in the south from its rocky ridges and bluffs in the north. Cypress swamps cover the western corner of the region.

The Western Coal Field lies in northwestern Kentucky. The region is surrounded on three sides by the Pennyroyal. About half of Kentucky's plentiful coal reserves are buried under the steep hills and fertile soil of the Western Coal Field.

Water is an abundant natural resource in Kentucky. In fact, Kentucky claims more miles of running water than any other state except

The Ohio River cuts a jagged border between Kentucky and Ohio.

Alaska. Ships travel on more than 1,000 miles (1,609 km) of these rivers, which serve as trade routes. Some of the most important rivers are the Ohio, Mississippi, Green, Kentucky, Licking, and Salt.

Of the many lakes scattered throughout Kentucky, some of the largest are artificial, formed by huge dams built on rivers. Besides creating lakes, dams help control water. They hold back rivers to keep them from overflowing after heavy rains. Dams create energy, too. When released through a dam, the river water creates a strong force, which turns giant engines that produce electricity.

Snow weighs down the branches of a tree along a creek near Louisville.

Plentiful rain fills the rivers and lakes of Kentucky and nourishes its crops and plant life. About 48 inches (122 centimeters) of rain falls in the state each year, mostly during the spring.

Although Kentucky's weather is generally mild, the state has four different seasons. Winter is cool and moist, with a few light snowfalls. Usually, the temperature stays above freezing, except in the mountains of the southeast. Summers in Kentucky are hot and humid, with temperatures averaging 77° F (25° C). Thunderstorms, and sometimes tornadoes, blow through the state in the spring and summer.

The state's rainy weather and rich soil provide the perfect environment for a wide variety of plant life. Thick forests of ash, beech, hickory, and oak blanket almost half of the state. Many flowering trees, such as the fragrant magnolia, are also found in Kentucky.

Deer abound in Kentucky's forests. Foxes, skunks, and mink also prowl in wooded areas, while raccoon, chipmunks, and opossums raise their young in fields, in forests, and even in city neighborhoods.

Barn owls *(above)* **nest in hollow trees and empty buildings around the state. Dogwoods** *(left)* **bloom over much of Kentucky in the spring.**

Kentucky's Story

Kentucky's earliest inhabitants hunted mammoths and mastodons, huge hairy elephants with great tusks and giant teeth. The ancestors of these hunters probably found their way to North America while following prey across the Bering Strait, a land bridge that once connected North America to Asia.

The hunters reached Kentucky about 12,000 years ago. As the weather got drier and big game animals died out, the Native Americans, or Indians, hunted smaller animals and gathered seeds, nuts, and fruits for food.

Some of these Indians stopped moving from place to place and settled in the north central part of Kentucky about 2,500 years ago. Called mound builders, they buried their dead in pits or tombs. Important people were buried with treasured objects, such as pottery. On top of the tombs, the Indians piled layer upon layer of dirt, creating large mounds.

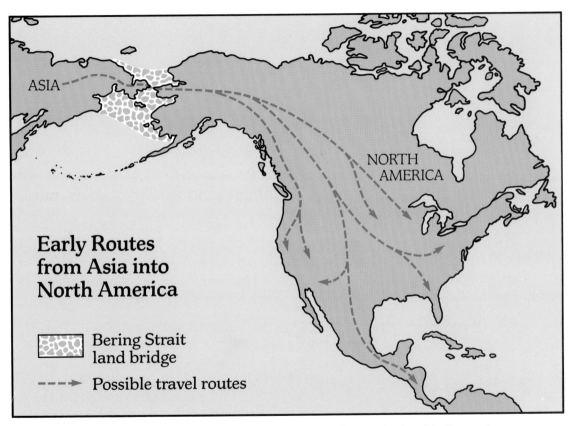

Early Routes from Asia into North America

ASIA

NORTH AMERICA

Bering Strait land bridge

----▶ Possible travel routes

The Indians who settled in the Kentucky area were descendants of Indians who probably came from Asia.

Some mound builders
made temple mounds as
well as burial mounds.
Here, a mound builder on
a temple mound
worships a god.

Using wood, mud, and grasses, the mound builders also built villages. They planted corn, beans, and squash to feed large populations. But by the early 1500s, the mound builders had disappeared. No one is sure what happened to them. Their crops may have failed because the weather became too dry or too cold.

The Woodland Indians were the next group to move to the area. Like the mound builders, these Indians were farmers. They built villages along Kentucky's many rivers.

But when the first Europeans ventured into the area in the 1600s, they found no Indian villages. The early Woodland Indians had moved away, and Kentucky had become a hunting ground shared by the Shawnee, Cherokee, and Iroquois tribes.

The Woodland Indians used spears and hooks to fish in rivers.

On Daniel Boone's second visit to Kentucky, in 1767, he brought a hunting party from North Carolina. The men lived in the wilderness of Kentucky for two years.

In 1750 Thomas Walker, an explorer, left his home in Virginia (one of the 13 British **colonies** in North America). He crossed into what is now eastern Kentucky through a low place, called a pass, in the Cumberland Mountains. Walker named the pass the Cumberland Gap. In 1774 James Harrod and a group of colonists followed Walker's path through the gap and established Harrodsburg, the first permanent white settlement in what would become Kentucky.

Not long afterward, Daniel Boone blazed a trail through the mountain forests of the Cumberland Gap. This path came to be called the Wilderness Road. Hundreds of people from the 13 colonies made their way west—to Kentucky and beyond—on that trail. The pioneers were looking for more land on which to build homes and farms.

The Shawnee and the Cherokee did not trust most of these pioneers. Most settlers showed little respect for the Indians and their hunting grounds. Fearful that the newcomers would take over the area, the Shawnee and Cherokee became hostile toward the settlers.

Kentucky's earliest pioneers built thick log walls around settlements for protection against Indian attacks.

The Indians and the settlers battled each other fiercely for the land. The Indians got many of their guns from the British, who were fighting the colonists in a war called the American Revolution (1775-1783). Armies of Indians, led by British commanders, fought against groups of settlers at Kentucky forts such as Boonesborough and Fort Harrod.

The colonists defeated the British in 1783 and formed their own country—the United States of America.

At meetings like this one, the Indians agreed to fight with the British against the colonists.

For many years, Virginians traveled through the Cumberland Gap to make new homes in Kentucky County.

Kentucky became a county, or section, of the state of Virginia.

Virginia encouraged people to move to its western land. Between 1783 and the early 1790s, almost 100,000 people traveled the Wilderness Road to reach Kentucky County. The county soon had enough people to apply for statehood, and by 1792 Kentucky had become the 15th state to join the Union.

Settlers in Kentucky had to cut down thick forests before they could build homes or plant crops.

The Shawnee and Cherokee still fought to regain their land, but more settlers kept coming. By 1794 the U.S. Army had pushed the Shawnee west to what is now Missouri and the Cherokee south to Tennessee and North Carolina. Few Indians remained in Kentucky.

Kentucky's rich farmland attracted more and more settlers. By 1800 the state's population had grown to 200,000 people. About one-fifth of these people were black slaves. Settlers from southern states brought the slaves to Kentucky to work in tobacco and corn fields.

Farming was how most Kentuckians made a living. Farmers used river routes to transport their products to market. Crops and livestock were shipped from Kentucky to ports along the Mississippi and Ohio rivers.

By 1840 Kentucky was leading the nation in the growing of hemp, a plant used to make rope. By 1860 Kentucky was growing more tobacco than any other state. When bourbon, a type of alcohol made from corn and invented in Kentucky, became popular among settlers, Kentuckians began growing more corn, too.

In 1829 Kentuckians built a canal around the Falls of the Ohio River, opening a waterway from Kentucky to New Orleans, Louisiana. Steamboats could now carry Kentucky's hemp, tobacco, and bourbon to markets along the Mississippi.

In 1860 most people who lived in the southern United States were farmers. Some of them, to make a profit, needed slaves to raise crops. Factories were more common than farms in the North, where more people lived in cities and didn't rely on slave labor.

Kentucky had strong ties to both the North and South. Almost all Kentuckians, like Southerners, still lived in the countryside and farmed the land. But many Kentuckians, like many Northerners, were opposed to slavery.

When Northerners began pushing Southerners to outlaw slavery, several Southern states decided to form a separate country that allowed slavery. They called their new nation the Confederate States of America. Kentuckians were torn. Should they join this new country with their Southern neighbors or stay in the Union with their Northern neighbors?

Kentuckians didn't want to choose sides in this conflict, which became known as the Civil War (1861–1865). But when both Union (Northern) and Confederate (Southern) troops invaded the state in 1861, Kentucky's government decided to stay in the Union. The state government forced Confederate troops to leave Kentucky.

In the Battle of Perryville in 1862, Confederate and Union troops fought for control of Kentucky. The Confederates lost and returned to their camps in Tennessee.

Still, many Kentuckians felt loyal to the South, and 35,000 of them fought for the Confederacy. More than twice as many Kentuckians fought for the North. When the Union won the war in 1865, however, it treated Kentucky as a defeated enemy. Union troops were sent to occupy sections of the state that had sided with the South.

Kentucky was heavily damaged by the war. Homes, crops, and livestock had been lost in battles. Army troops had destroyed most of the state's transportation systems and nearly all of its schools.

After the Civil War, some Kentuckians joined a group called the Ku Klux Klan. The Klan attacked black people and Union supporters, sometimes beating them or setting their homes on fire.

The Hatfields and the McCoys

The Hatfield family

Oftentimes, friends, neighbors, and family members in Kentucky fought on opposite sides during the Civil War. This sometimes caused feuds, or fights, that lasted long after the war ended. One of Kentucky's most famous feuds was between the McCoys from Kentucky and the Hatfields who lived nearby in West Virginia.

Over the years, many stories have been told about the feuding. One tale says that the trouble began in 1863 when a soldier from the pro-Union McCoy family was found dead near the Hatfields' home. The McCoys thought that the Hatfields, who were Confederates, had killed the soldier. To get even, the McCoys killed a Hatfield.

The fighting grew worse in 1882 when a Hatfield man and a McCoy woman tried to elope, or run away to get married secretly. Their families caught them. In the battle that followed, a Hatfield got shot. Later, three McCoy brothers were found murdered.

A small-scale war between the families followed. At least 20 and possibly as many as 100 people were killed before the feuding ended in the 1890s.

Kentuckians labored to rebuild their state. Farmers replanted their fields, while shopkeepers restocked their stores. Kentucky's traders went to the South, where people had suffered even more losses in the war and needed Kentucky's goods and crops.

Coal production, like trade, increased steadily after the war. Throughout the country, thousands of factories were built, and they needed coal to run their machinery. Kentucky began producing more coal than almost any other state.

Tobacco continued to be an important source of money for Kentucky, gradually replacing hemp as the number one crop. Louisville became the world's largest tobacco market, with traders buying and selling tobacco leaves and tobacco products.

In the early 1900s, most Kentuckians still lived on small farms. These families raised most of their own food. Hunting and fishing added meat to the family table.

The Louisville and Nashville
Railroad *(left)* linked Kentucky to
markets in the South. The
railroad carried coal,
manufactured goods, and crops
such as hemp *(below)*.

The Black Patch War

In the early 1900s, Kentucky's farmers grew more tobacco than farmers in almost every other state. Big tobacco companies made lots of money selling tobacco products, such as cigarettes and cigars, nationwide. But the American Tobacco Company of Kentucky wanted to make even more money. The company started to offer farmers low prices for their tobacco crops. Before long, American Tobacco convinced other companies to bid the same low rate.

Angry farmers in southwestern Kentucky banded together and refused to sell their tobacco so cheaply. Some farmers, however, continued to sell tobacco for the low price. They said they couldn't afford to stop selling their crops altogether.

To stop these tobacco sales, a group of farmers formed the Night Riders in 1905. For the next four years, the riders went out after dark to burn the fields and barns of the farmers who kept selling their crops.

These raids became known as the Black Patch War because the Night Riders grew dark-leafed tobacco. Kentucky's government sent army troops to the area in 1909 and stopped the Night Riders. But the farmers won—companies began to pay higher tobacco prices once again.

By the early 1900s, Kentuckians could earn more money as coal miners than they had earned as farmers. But mining was dangerous. Many miners died in accidents and almost all miners developed lung diseases from breathing coal dust.

World War I (1914–1918) changed the lives of Kentucky's farmers. The war created a high demand for coal to fuel the factories that made weapons. Mining towns sprang up near Kentucky's coal fields as farmers left their homes to dig for the mineral. But the mining boom ended with the war. Most miners, who had sold their farms to work in the mines, lost their jobs and their only source of money.

One of the worst floods of the Ohio River in recorded history happened in 1937. Cities all along the river's banks were flooded, and nearly a million people were left homeless. Schools were closed for more than a month.

More people lost their jobs in the 1930s, during a period called the Great Depression. Many banks and businesses shut down. But during World War II (1939–1945), coal was needed once more and mining again employed thousands of Kentuckians. Meanwhile, new factories were being built in Louisville and Lexington, creating jobs for the rural Kentuckians who were moving to the cities.

Many Kentuckians in Louisville and Lexington worked in tobacco warehouses, either bundling the leaves for sale or selling them to tobacco companies.

The pioneer and the politician on Kentucky's flag represent the people who worked to make Kentucky a state. The flag pictured was made official in 1962.

At the same time, the state began to change the way it treated African Americans. Black people in many states, including Kentucky, had not been allowed to go to the same schools or hospitals as white people. Many businesses would hire only white workers.

During the 1950s and 1960s, African Americans protested the way they were treated and demonstrated for their **civil rights,** or personal freedoms. In 1966 Kentucky became the first southern state to pass a law that said employers could not refuse to hire workers because of the color of their skin.

Troops in Kentucky guarded the streets of Louisville during some civil rights protests.

| 10,000 B.C. | 500 B.C. | A.D. 1500 | 1750 | 1774 | 1792 |

Native American hunters reach what is now Kentucky

Mound builders arrive in Kentucky and build villages

Woodland Indians farm near the Ohio River

Thomas Walker finds the Cumberland Gap

Harrodsburg is founded

Kentucky becomes the 15th state

By 1970, for the first time in the state's history, more Kentuckians were living in cities and towns than in rural areas. This was an important change, but many other changes have also shaped Kentucky. Native Americans no longer hunt mammoths, and pioneers no longer travel the Wilderness Road. The first trails marked in Kentucky are now old, but Kentuckians keep blazing new trails.

40

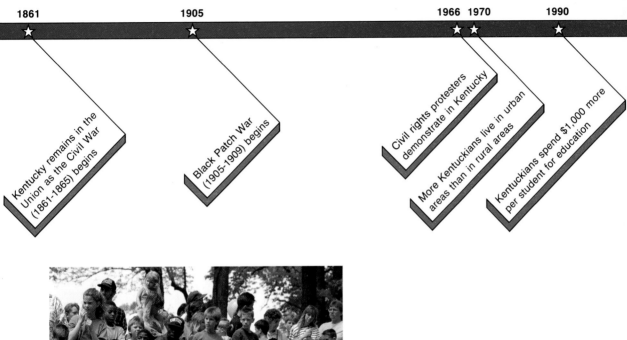

1861 — Kentucky remains in the Union as the Civil War (1861-1865) begins

1905 — Black Patch War (1905-1909) begins

1966 — Civil rights protesters demonstrate in Kentucky

1970 — More Kentuckians live in urban areas than in rural areas

1990 — Kentuckians spend $1,000 more per student for education

In 1990 Kentuckians voted to spend more money for each schoolchild in the state.

Living and Working in Kentucky

Though Kentucky still has the blue-grass fields and rolling mountains Daniel Boone loved, he probably wouldn't want to live in the state today. According to Boone, elbow room meant not being able to see the smoke from his neighbors' chimneys. Kentucky's population has grown so much that Boone would have trouble finding that kind of elbow room.

The lights of Louisville reflect off of the Ohio River.

More than 3.5 million people call Kentucky home. About half of them live in urban areas, or cities. Kentucky's largest urban center is Louisville, followed by Lexington, Owensboro, Covington, Bowling Green, and Paducah. Except for Lexington and Bowling Green, all of these cities lie along the southern bank of the Ohio River.

Racehorses leap out of the gates at the Keeneland Race Course.

Though most Kentuckians were born in the United States, their ancestors came from England, Scotland, Ireland, France, Germany, and various African nations. Seven percent of the state's population is black. People from Central and South American countries make up an even smaller part of Kentucky's population.

Kentuckians are famous for many things, including racehorses. Many people in the state make a living by raising and selling Thoroughbreds. In the Bluegrass Region, horse lovers can stroll through horse farms, ride ponies at the Kentucky Horse Park, or watch the races at the Keeneland Race Course in Lexington. The Kentucky Derby, a horse race that has been run on Louisville's Churchill Downs since 1875, draws thousands of onlookers every May.

A bluegrass musician picks a tune on his mandolin.

Kentucky is also known for its bluegrass music. Banjos, fiddles, harmonicas, and mandolins are common bluegrass instruments. Kentuckian Bill Monroe and his Blue Grass Boys first performed this folk music just before World War II. Now bluegrass bands entertain people at festivals and celebrations all over the state.

Kentucky has large national forests and state parks that draw many visitors to the state each year. Some visitors hike through Daniel Boone National Forest. Others ride down the Big South Fork of the Cumberland River on rafts. Tourists can also visit historic forts and homes, such as Old Fort Harrod at Harrodsburg—Kentucky's oldest town.

With more than 300 miles (483 km) of passages, Mammoth Cave in central Kentucky is part of the world's longest cave system. Here, visitors can tour the huge underground caverns of Crystal Lake, have lunch in the Snowball Dining Room, or squeeze through the narrow passages of Fat Man's Misery. On one tour, visitors can even float in a boat down the underground Echo River.

Canoeists paddle down a Kentucky creek.

47

Louisville, one of the state's cultural centers, offers an orchestra, a ballet, an opera, and the nationally famous Actors Theater. Lexington has its own orchestra and holds a bluegrass music festival every summer.

As basketball fans around the country know, Louisville and Lexington are home to rival college basketball teams. The University of Louisville's Cardinals and the University of Kentucky's Wildcats draw large crowds from around the state. Kentucky's baseball fans cheer for the Louisville Redbirds, a minor-league baseball team.

A Cardinal leaps to grab the basketball.

More than two-thirds of Kentucky's workers perform service jobs. Some of these workers teach students or care for sick people. Others sell clothes, food, or cars. Two military bases, Forts Knox and Campbell, employ thousands of soldiers and other service workers.

Kentuckians work at all kinds of service jobs, from transporting coal *(left)* to helping tourists at resorts *(above)*.

For generations, Kentuckians have been aging bourbon in oak barrels.

Coal and oil, found in the Eastern and Western coal fields, are the state's most valuable minerals. Although only 2 percent of Kentuckians work in mining, this industry brings in 12 percent of all the state's money.

A little more than one-fifth, or 20 percent, of all money earned in Kentucky comes from manufacturing. Workers make a lot of bourbon, a whiskey named after a county in central Kentucky. In fact, Kentucky makes more bourbon than any other state. Louisville processes more tobacco than anywhere else in the world. People make the dried tobacco leaves into cigarettes and other tobacco products. Workers in the state also make tractors, cars and trucks, mobile homes, air conditioners, paint, and typewriters.

At some car factories in Kentucky, robots put the automobiles together.

Kentuckians earn more money from tobacco than from any other crop.

Tobacco, of course, grows on many of Kentucky's farms. Besides tobacco, farmers harvest soybeans, corn, and wheat. Others breed horses or raise cattle. Kentuckians also enjoy homegrown apples, peaches, and the famous popcorn of Calloway County.

A soldier shows off his helmet to a friend, who might someday become a soldier too.

Despite its many farms, Kentucky is no longer mainly a farming state. Agriculture employs only 7 percent of the state's workers. Kentucky still has miles of rich farmland, but its people can now choose from many different kinds of work.

Protecting the Environment

Kentucky has many valuable natural resources, including water and soil. But one of the state's most profitable natural resources is coal. Kentucky's coal miners earned more than $1 billion in 1988. That same year, they produced about 161 million tons (146 million metric tons) of coal.

More than one-third of Kentucky's coal is uncovered by **surface mining**. Surface miners scrape or blast off the tops of hills and mountains to expose the coal underneath. They strip away trees and topsoil, leaving ugly scars.

Surface mining not only destroys the beauty of the land but also ruins farmland and pollutes rivers and streams. By removing the protective trees and plants from the soil, surface mining also causes **erosion.** In this process, wind and rain carry the exposed soil around the mine into clear streams, turning the streams to mud. Erosion can also cause landslides that destroy homes and more land.

Surface miners cut rock, soil, and trees from hills to reach Kentucky's coal.

Until 1977 few laws protected the land from the effects of surface mining. But the Surface Mining Control and Reclamation Act of 1977 changed that. The law requires that surface-mine owners

Acid collects in pools of water at abandoned mines. Rain carries the acidic water into nearby streams and rivers, where the acid kills fish and plants.

Miners reclaim mined land by replanting it with trees and flowers.

practice **reclamation**—that is, they must reclaim, or restore, land damaged by surface mines. To do this, mine owners put soil back onto the mine, plant trees and grasses, and leave the land at least as useful as it was before mining began.

To make sure that miners follow the law, the state government charges mine operators a fee before they begin mining. Mine operators get that money back once they have completed the mining and reclaimed the stripped land. If an operator does not do a good job of restoring the mine, the government keeps the fee and uses that money to rebuild the stripped area.

Government inspectors try to make sure that everyone follows the reclamation laws, but surface mining remains a problem. The law does not require surface mines dug before 1977 to be reclaimed. And until 1987, surface mines of two acres (one hectare) or less didn't have to be reclaimed either.

Reclamation can be expensive, and many mine operators do not want to pay for it. To avoid paying for reclamation, some people operate small, hidden mines in Kentucky. These miners, called **wildcatters,** secretly mine coal and then leave the area without rebuilding the stripped land.

Surface-mining inspectors fly over coal fields in helicopters looking for wildcatters, but illegal mining is still common in Kentucky. When inspectors find illegal mines, the wildcatters are brought to court. But they often avoid paying fines.

Wildcatters strip the soil off a coal mine.

Wildcatters dig coal from a mine *(right)*. The miners then hide their bulldozers in nearby forests *(below)* so that surface-mining inspectors won't spy the equipment from their helicopters.

59

Trees replace bare soil on reclaimed coal mines.

Local judges and juries sometimes choose not to enforce the reclamation laws. The courts know that some wildcatters turn to illegal mining because they can't find any other work. And once the damage to the land is done, many wildcatters claim they cannot afford to reclaim the land they have mined. So the wildcatters go free.

But the state is making progress. Many mining companies do an excellent job of restoring the land. The state's Department for Surface Mining Reclamation and Enforcement is hard at work repairing old mine sites and stopping further damage. Kentucky's coal deposits are expected to last another 200 years, so reclaiming mine sites will be an important job for years to come.

When miners reclaim mined land, they sometimes make the area more useful than it was before. They use the soil they removed from the mine to fill in nearby valleys and turn the stripped landscape into rolling pastures and farmland.

Kentucky's Famous People

ACTIVISTS

Mary Breckinridge (1881–1965) moved to Leslie County, Kentucky, in the 1920s. She created the Frontier Nursing Service, a group of health-care clinics that brought doctors and nurses to rural mountain families.

Whitney Moore Young, Jr. (1921–1971), born in Lincoln Ridge, Kentucky, was a civil rights leader. Young worked to get job training, quality education, and decent housing for black people. He was the director of the National Urban League from 1961 to 1971.

▲ MARY BRECKINRIDGE

▲ WHITNEY YOUNG

◄ JIM VARNEY

ENID YANDELL ▶

ACTORS & ARTISTS

Edward Troye (1808–1874) was born in Switzerland but spent most of his adult life in Kentucky and the South painting portraits of famous Thoroughbred horses. His horse portraits were considered the best of the 1800s.

Jim Varney (born 1949) is an actor and comedian from Lexington. He began his career making commercials and has played the part of Ernest in the motion pictures *Ernest Saves Christmas* and *Ernest Goes to Camp.*

Enid Yandell (1870–1934), a sculptor, was born in Louisville. Her works of art are displayed throughout Kentucky and other states. Yandell was the first female member of the National Sculpture Society.

Muhammad Ali (Cassius Clay) (born 1942), from Louisville, first became the Heavyweight Boxing Champion of the World in 1964, after only 20 fights. He earned the same title two more times before retiring in 1979.

Harold Henry "Pee Wee" Reese (born 1919) played shortstop for the Brooklyn Dodgers in the 1940s and 1950s. Reese, from Elkton, Kentucky, was elected to the National Baseball Hall of Fame in 1984.

Adolph Rupp (1910–1977) played basketball for the University of Kansas but gained his greatest fame later, as a basketball coach at the University of Kentucky. Rupp, who coached from 1930 to 1972, led the Wildcats to 875 wins—more than any other college basketball coach has won.

▲ MUHAMMAD ALI

▲ HAROLD REESE

▲ DUNCAN HINES

COLONEL SANDERS ▶

Duncan Hines (1880–1959) was born in Bowling Green, Kentucky. From 1936 to 1959 he wrote national restaurant guidebooks called *Adventures in Good Eating*. He later gained more fame when his name became a brand name for packaged foods.

Colonel Harland Sanders (1890–1980), owner of Sanders' Cafe in Corbin, Kentucky, founded Kentucky Fried Chicken, a fastfood restaurant, in 1956. Sanders was made an honorary colonel by the governor of Kentucky in 1935.

George Ella Lyon (born 1949) grew up in Harlan, Kentucky—a mountain coal town that probably gave her ideas for her children's books. She has written *Red Rover, Red Rover; Borrowed Children;* and *Come a Tide.*

Diane Sawyer (born 1945) is a television journalist. Born in Glasgow, Kentucky, Sawyer was the first female reporter on "60 Minutes." She co-hosts the television news show "Prime Time Live."

Robert Penn Warren (1905–1989) was a novelist, poet, teacher, and literary critic from Guthrie, Kentucky. He won three Pulitzer prizes and earned the title poet laureate, or outstanding poet, of the United States in 1986.

▲ GEORGE ELLA LYON

◄ CRYSTAL GAYLE

LORETTA LYNN ▶

MUSICIANS

"Red" Foley (1910–1968), of Bluelick, Kentucky, has been called the founder of country music. Foley was made a member of the Country Music Hall of Fame in 1967.

Crystal Gayle (born 1951) is a country music singer from Paintsville, Kentucky. The sister of Loretta Lynn, Gayle won a Grammy Award for her song "Don't It Make My Brown Eyes Blue."

Loretta Lynn (born 1935), a country music singer from Butcher Hollow, Kentucky, was the first woman to receive the Entertainer of the Year award from the Country Music Association. Lynn has recorded many hit songs, including "Coal Miner's Daughter." Her autobiography of the same name was made into a movie.

Daniel Boone (1734–1820) first saw Kentucky on a hunting trip. He returned with other pioneers and built Boonesborough— one of Kentucky's first white settlements. Although Boone died in Missouri, he is buried in Frankfort, Kentucky.

DANIEL ▶
BOONE

CASSIUS ▶
CLAY

▲ HENRY
CLAY

ZACHARY ▶
TAYLOR

POLITICIANS

Cassius Marcellus Clay (1810–1903), of Madison County, Kentucky, was an antislavery activist and politician. He served in the Kentucky legislature and founded an antislavery paper, the *True American.*

Henry Clay (1777–1852) began his political career in the Kentucky state legislature in 1803. He then served in the U.S. Senate and as the U.S. secretary of state. He was known as the Great Compromiser for his skill at settling arguments.

Zachary Taylor (1784–1850), who grew up near Louisville, served as the twelfth U.S. president from 1849 to 1850. Nicknamed Old Rough-and-Ready, Taylor became a national war hero when he fought in the Mexican War (1846–1848).

Facts-at-a-Glance

Nickname: Bluegrass State
Song: "My Old Kentucky Home"
Motto: United We Stand,
  Divided We Fall
Flower: goldenrod
Tree: Kentucky coffee tree
Bird: Kentucky cardinal

Population: 3,685,296*
Rank in population, nationwide: 23rd
Area: 40,409 sq mi (104,659 sq km)
Rank in area, nationwide: 37th
Date and ranking of statehood:
  June 1, 1792, the 15th state
Capital: Frankfort (25,968*)
Major cities (and populations*):
  Louisville (269,063), Lexington-Fayette
  (225,366), Owensboro (53,549), Covington
  (43,264), Bowling Green (40,641)
U.S. senators: 2
U.S. representatives: 6
Electoral votes: 8

* 1990 census

Places to visit: Land Between the Lakes near Paducah, Schmidt's Museum of Coca-Cola Memorabilia in Elizabethtown, Kentucky Horse Park in Lexington, Red River Gorge Geologic Area in Daniel Boone National Forest, Big Bone Lick State Park near Union

Annual events: Bar-B-Q Festival in Owensboro (May), High School Basketball Tournament in Louisville or Lexington (March), Kentucky Derby Festival in Louisville (May), Shaker Heritage Weekends Festival near Harrodsburg (Sept.), International Banana Festival in Fulton (Aug.)

Average January temperature: 34° F (1° C)	Average July temperature: 77° F (25° C)

Natural resources: fertile soil, coal, petroleum, natural gas, limestone, lakes and rivers, clays, fluorite, lead, sand and gravel

Agricultural products: Thoroughbred horses, tobacco, beef, milk, soybeans, peaches, apples, popcorn

Manufactured goods: air conditioners, typewriters, tractors, bourbon whiskey, tobacco products, paint, plastics

ENDANGERED SPECIES

Mammals—mountain lion, evening bat, long-tailed shrew, New England cottontail, black bear

Birds—spotted sandpiper, American bittern, lark sparrow, blackburnian warbler

Reptiles—Kirtland's snake, southern coal skink, coachwhip, green water snake

Fish—alligator gar, pallid shiner, blotchside logperch, southern brook lamprey

Plants—Barbara's buttons, hair grass, fringed loosestrife, sunflower, beardgrass, burhead

WHERE KENTUCKIANS WORK

Services—46 percent
  (services includes jobs in trade; community, social, & personal services; finance, insurance, & real estate; transportation, communication, & utilities)
Manufacturing—24 percent
Government—17 percent
Agriculture—7 percent
Construction—4 percent
Mining—2 percent

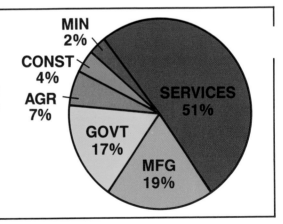

MIN 2%
CONST 4%
AGR 7%
SERVICES 51%
GOVT 17%
MFG 19%

PRONUNCIATION GUIDE

Appalachian Plateau
  (ap-uh-LAY-chuhn pla-TOH)

Bering Strait (BEHR-ihng STRAYT)

Cherokee (CHER-uh-kee)

Iroquois (IHR-uh-kwoy)

Lexington (LEHK-sing-tuhn)

Louisville (LOO-ih-vihl)

New Orleans (noo OR-lee-uhns)

Owensboro (OH-uhnz-buhr-uh)

Paducah (puh-DOO-kuh)

Shawnee (shaw-NEE)

Glossary

civil rights The right of all citizens—regardless of race, religion, sex—to enjoy life, liberty, property, and equal protection under the law.

colony A territory ruled by a country some distance away.

erosion The wearing away of the earth's surface by the forces of water, wind, or ice.

knob A small, rounded hill or mountain.

plateau A large, relatively flat area that stands above the surrounding land.

reclamation The process of rebuilding land that has been mined and making it usable for plants, animals, or people.

surface mining A method of mining minerals that lie near the surface of the earth. Dirt, rock, and other materials are removed to uncover the mineral.

swamp A wetland permanently soaked with water. Woody plants (trees and shrubs) are the main form of vegetation in a swamp.

wildcatter In Kentucky, a miner who takes coal from the ground illegally, without getting permission to mine.

Index

ACKNOWLEDGEMENTS:

Maryland Cartographics, pp. 2, 10; © 1992 Adam Jones, pp. 2–3, 7, 21, 42; Jack Lindstrom, p. 6; © 1992 Daniel E. Dempster, pp. 8, 16, 41, 44–45, 46, 49 (bottom), 53, 61; Maslowski Photo, p. 11; Kent & Donna Dannen, pp. 12, 13; Kentucky Department of Travel Development, pp. 14, 17 (bottom), 69; Monica V. Brown, Photographic Artist, p. 15; TVA photo by Ed Ray, p. 17 (top); Laura Westlund, pp. 19, 38; Tennessee State Museum, from a painting by Carlyle Urello, p. 20; The Filson Club, pp. 22, 23, 24, 26, 29, 34, 36; Virginia State Library and Archives, p. 25; R. G. Potter Collection, Photographic Archives, University of Louisville, p. 27; Bettman Archives, pp. 30, 39; Library of Congress, pp. 31, 65 (bottom right); The Kentucky Library, Western Kentucky University, pp. 32–33, 37; Arthur Y. Ford Albums, Photographic Archives, University of Louisville, p. 33; Canfield & Shark Collection, Photographic Archives, University of Louisville, p. 35; John Nation / Louisville Convention and Visitors Bureau, p. 43; Kentucky Department of Parks, pp. 47, 49 (top); Louisville Convention and Visitors Bureau, p. 48; Owensboro-Daviess County Tourist Commission, p. 50; Toyota Motor Manufacturing U.S.A., Inc., p. 51; Carol Barrett, p. 52; Charles Bertram, p. 54; Thomas Spellman, Office of Special Investigations, Kentucky, N.R.E.P.C., pp. 56, 58, 59 (top and bottom); Kay Shaw, pp. 57, 71; Kentucky Division of Forestry, p. 60; Photographic Archives, Alice Lloyd College, p. 62 (top left); Independent Picture Service, pp. 62 (top right), 65 (top, center); Hollywood Book & Poster Company, p. 62 (bottom left); Illinois State University, p. 62 (bottom right); The Ring Magazine, p. 63 (top left); National Baseball Library, Cooperstown, N.Y., p. 63 (top right); Duncan Hines, p. 63 (bottom left); Kentucky Fried Chicken, p. 63 (bottom right); Orchard Books, p. 64 (top); Janice Smith, p. 64 (bottom left); Loretta Lynn Enterprises, p. 64 (bottom right); Virginia State Library and Archives, p. 65 (bottom left); Library of Congress, p. 65 (bottom right); Jean Matheny, p. 66